Alligator
in an
Anorak

A Random House book
Published by Random House Australia Pty Ltd
Level 3, 100 Pacific Highway, North Sydney NSW 2060
www.randomhouse.com.au

First published by Random House Australia in 2014

Addresses for companies within the Random House Group can be found at
www.randomhouse.com.au/offices

National Library of Australia
Cataloguing-in-Publication Entry

Author: Parton, Daron, author.
Title: Alligator in an anorak / Daron Parton.
ISBN: 978 0 85798 309 1 (hardback)
Target Audience: For children.
Subjects: English language – Alphabet – Juvenile literature.
        Alphabet books – Juvenile literature.
        Animals – Juvenile literature.
Dewey Number: 421.1

Cover illustration by Daron Parton
Cover design by Alicia Freile/Tango Media
Internal design by Alicia Freile/Tango Media

Printed in China by 1010 Printing International Co. Ltd.

Alligator
in an
Anorak

Daron Parton

RANDOM HOUSE AUSTRALIA

Alligator in an Anorak

Bear in a Bathtub

Crab in a Caravan

Dodo in a **Dive**

Elephant in an Eggcup

Fish in a Fountain

Giraffe in Galoshes

Hippo in a Helicopter

Ibis in an Igloo

Jackdaw in a Jar

Kangaroo in a Kayak

Lion in a Letterbox

Mole in the Middle

Newt in a Necktie

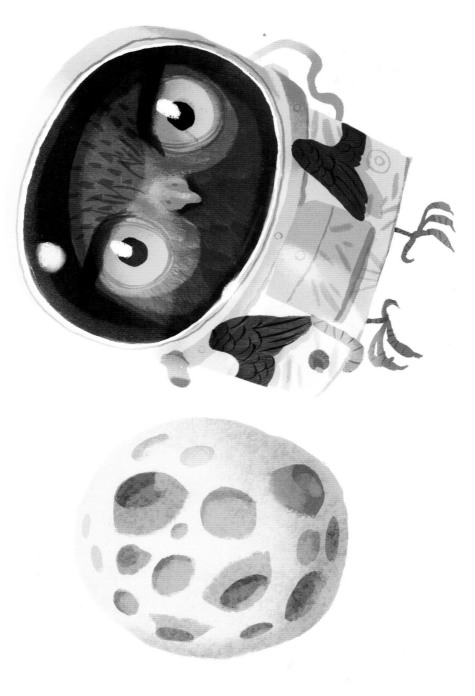

Owl in Orbit

Panda in a Paper hat

Quail in a Quartet

Rhino in a Rocket

Snake in a Sock

Tiger in a Tent

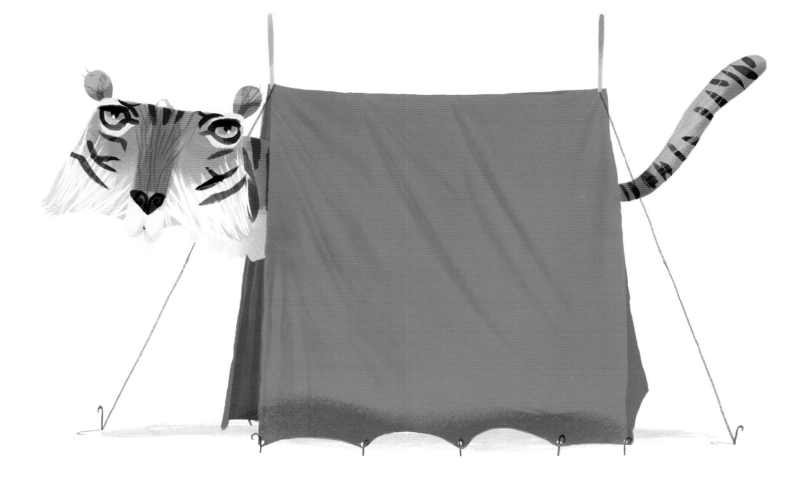

Urchin in Undies

Vulture in Venice

Whale in a Wigwam

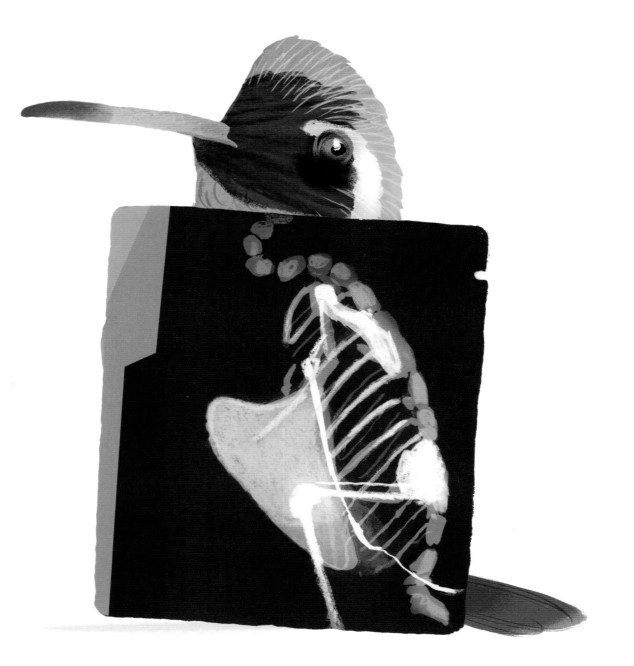

Xantus in an **X-ray**

Yak in a Yacht

Zebra in a Zoo